Harriet
the Elephotamus

Written by Fiona Kirkman

Illustrated by Dawn Treacher

Stairwell Books ///

Harriet looked at her reflection in the watering hole.

She might look like a hippopotamus, but ever since she could remember she felt like an elephant.

She didn't like wallowing in the mud or lazing in the water like her brothers and sisters.

She often watched the elephants and wished she could be with them.
So one day she decided to go and ask the elephant herd if she could live with them and be an elephant.

She set off very excited.

"Where are you going?"
said Chimp.

"I am not a hippopotamus. I am an elephant,
so I am going to join the herd,"
she said, with head
held high.

Chimp laughed.

"You aren't an elephant, Harriet, look at your nose."

"The herd will laugh you off the plain."

"Come along if you want," said Harriet.

But no more laughing at me."

Inside she started to worry. What if they sent her away?

"Where are you going?" chirped Sandpiper.

"She says she is really an elephant, not a hippopotamus, and is going to live with the herd," said chimp.

Sandpiper laughed and laughed.

"Ooh! Can I come along too?" Sandpiper chirped.

"You are not an elephant, Harriet, look at your ears."

Sandpiper pecked an insect from behind Harriet's ear and she giggled.

It always tickled her.

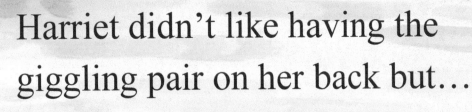

Harriet didn't like having the
giggling pair on her back but…

she was happy to have company
on her journey.

"Where are you going?" asked Giraffe.

"She is really an elephant and is going to live with the herd," Chimp and Sandpiper said together.

"WHAT?!" said Giraffe.

He bent his head down, thinking he had misheard.

Giraffe laughed.

"Does that make you an elephotamus?"

Everyone laughed, even Harriet.

When they arrived at the clearing, Harriet suddenly felt very small and scared.

What if they laughed at her?

She couldn't go back to the watering hole, she didn't belong there.

Where could an elephotamus live?

She took a deep breath and started to head towards the herd.

The elephants turned to watch.

It wasn't everyday a hippopotamus,
a chimp, a sandpiper and a giraffe
were seen together on
the plains.

"What do you want?" boomed the biggest female of the herd.

Harriet decided it was now or never.

"I'm Harriet. I know I look like a hippopotamus but I have always known I am really an elephant."

"She is an elephotamus," Chimp, Sandpiper and Giraffe giggled, waiting for the elephants to laugh too.

But they didn't.

The female elephant was very quiet.

"I want to live with the herd and be a real elephant," whispered Harriet.

The elephant looked at her herd and flapped her ears and they all turned and started to walk away.

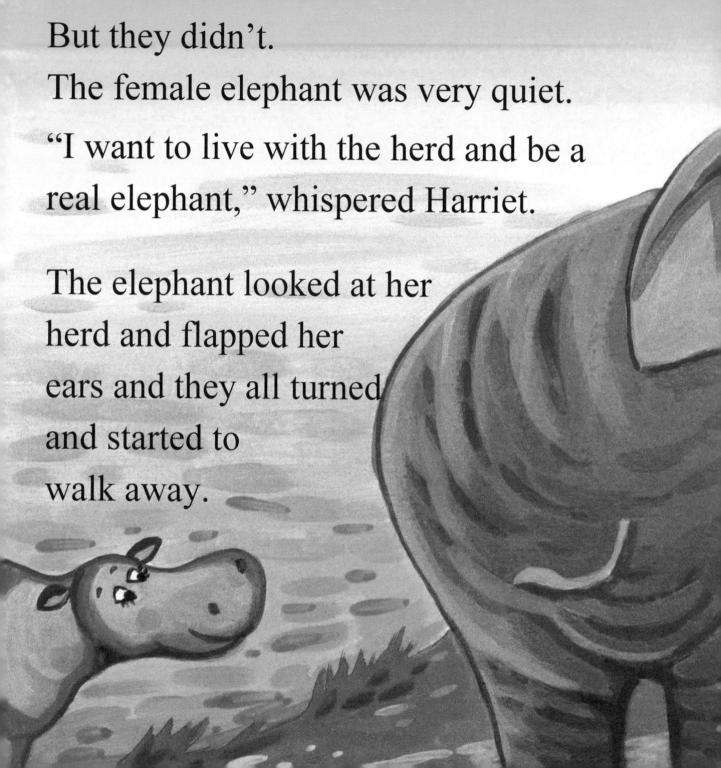

"Well, you had better keep up!"
the elephant shouted back at Harriet.

A small elephant came from the back
of the herd.

"You can walk with me,
Harriet,
if you want."

Chimp, Sandpiper and Giraffe watched Harriet leave with the herd and they felt bad they had made fun of their friend.

All together they shouted, "Good luck Harriet."

If you ever see a hippotamus with a herd
of elephants, you never know,
it might just be…

Harriet the elephotamus.

For Daniel.

Published by Stairwell Books
161 Lowther Street
York, YO31 7LZ

ISBN: 978-1-913432-32-4

Layout design: Alan Gillott
Cover art: Dawn Treacher
P4

www.stairwellbooks.co.uk
@stairwellbooks

Also available from Stairwell Books:

Mouse Pirate written and Illustrated by Dawn Treacher

Lightning Source UK Ltd.
Milton Keynes UK
UKHW050830171121
394107UK00003B/16